Groundhog Day

For Dave Epstein
—M. M.

ALADDIN PAPERBACKS
An imprint of Simon & Schuster Children's Publishing Division
1230 Avenue of the Americas, New York, NY 10020
Text copyright © 2006 by Brenda Bowen
Illustrations copyright © 2006 by Mike Gordon
All rights reserved, including the right of reproduction in whole or in part in any form.
READY-TO-READ is a registered trademark of Simon & Schuster, Inc.
ALADDIN PAPERBACKS and colophon are trademarks of Simon & Schuster, Inc.
Designed by Sammy Yuen Jr.
The text of this book was set in CentSchBook BT.
Manufactured in the United States of America
First Aladdin Paperbacks edition January 2006
4   6   8   10   9   7   5   3
Library of Congress Cataloging-in-Publication Data
McNamara, Margaret.
Groundhog Day / Margaret McNamara ;
illustrated by Mike Gordon.—1st Aladdin Paperbacks ed.
p. cm.—(Ready-to-read) (Robin Hill School)
Summary: On Groundhog Day, the students in Mrs. Connor's class try to find out
whether the class hamster can predict the weather as well as a groundhog.
ISBN-13: 978-1-4169-0507-3 (Aladdin pbk.)
ISBN-10: 1-4169-0507-3 (Aladdin pbk.)
ISBN-13: 978-1-4169-0508-0 (library edition)
ISBN-10: 1-4169-0508-1 (library edition)
[1. Groundhog Day—Fiction. 2. Hamsters—Fiction. 3. Schools—Fiction.]
I. Gordon, Mike, ill. II. Title. III. Series.
PZ7.M232518Gro 2006
[E]—dc22
2005006578

Groundhog Day

Written by Margaret McNamara
Illustrated by Mike Gordon

Ready-to-Read
Aladdin Paperbacks
New York   London   Toronto   Sydney

One morning,
Mrs. Connor wrote a poem
on the blackboard.

If the sun shines bright
on Groundhog Day,
The snow will swirl
<u>until</u> it is May.

If the snow blows hard
on Groundhog Day,
The sun will shine
<u>before</u> it is May.

"Today is February second," said Mrs. Connor.

"Winter began six weeks ago."

"Winter will end six weeks
from now.
We are halfway
through winter."

Valentine

"But what is
Groundhog Day?"
asked Ayanna.

Jamie raised his hand.

"If on this day,"
Jamie said,
"a groundhog can see
his shadow, we will have
six more weeks of winter.

"But if a groundhog
CANNOT see his shadow,
then spring will come soon."

"That is crazy,"
said Michael.

"Crazy, but fun,"
said Mrs. Connor.

Mrs. Connor set a small
cage on her desk.

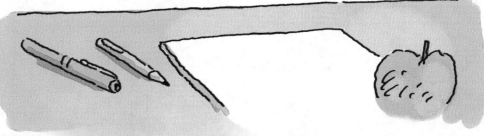

"Is that a groundhog?"
said Hannah.
"No," said Becky.
"That is a hamster!"

"His name is Chester,"
said Mrs. Connor.
"He will be our groundhog
today."

Mrs. Connor took Chester
to the windowsill.

"Chester will see
his shadow for sure,"
said Reza.
"I do not want any more
winter!" said Emma.

Mrs. Connor opened
the door to Chester's cage.
Chester looked up
and sniffed.

Chester slipped out of
his cage.

He looked around.

"No shadow!" cried Katie.
"No more winter!" said
Emma.

"Chester is not always right," said Mrs. Connor.

But that year,
that bright, sunny year,
he was.